SNUGGLES

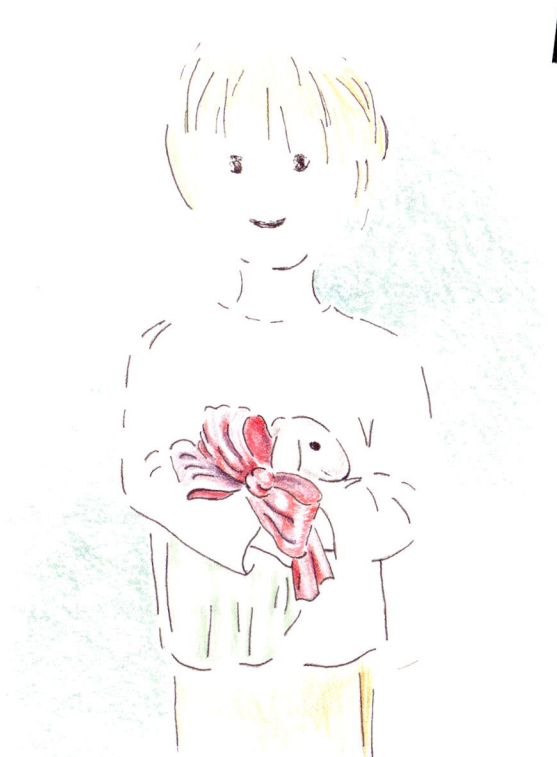

The bunny who helped me find God

by Myra T. Johnson

Conciliar Press Ministries, Inc.
Ben Lomond California

Snuggles: The Bunny Who Helped Me Find God
Text and illustrations © copyright 2007 by Myra T. Johnson

All rights reserved.

Published by   Conciliar Press Ministries, Inc.
              P.O. Box 76
              Ben Lomond, California 95005

Printed in China

ISBN 10: 1-888212-89-6
ISBN 13: 978-1-888212-89-1

"Stand still and consider the wondrous works of God."
—Job 37:14

Acknowledgements:

May God's mercy and blessing be with everyone who helped Snuggles and I along the great journey that this little book describes, with those who inspired me to write the story, and with those who have made its publication possible. I am deeply grateful to:

• Everyone at Conciliar Press, especially my Project Managing Editor, Jane Meyer; Production Editor, Carla Zell; Marketing Editor, Shelly Stamps; Ginny Nieuwsma and Father Thomas Zell.
• Megan George, for her photograph of Snuggles, and Roy Helo, of Lifetouch Portrait Studio, for the author's photograph.
• Irving Street Veterinary Hospital, in San Francisco, CA, for their excellent treatment of Snuggles over many years.
• Everyone at Saint Nicholas Orthodox Church in San Francisco, California, especially Rev. Father Nicholas Borzghol, Pastor, and congregants Nader and Sawsan Shatara and Isa and Christie Khayat. (The anticipated births of the Shatara and Khayat children, Nikola Shatara, and Alfred and Andrew Khayat, inspired me to write this book.)
• The congregation of Holy Trinity Orthodox Cathedral in San Francisco, California, especially the late Very Rev. Victor Sokolov (may his memory be eternal), and my godparents, Xenia and Ron Osedach.
• Father Stephen, whose wise counsel encouraged me to embrace my Faith.

The real Snuggles

Saint Nicholas Church in San Francisco, the Church I entered on a rainy day long ago.

Hi! I'm Snuggles, and I'm adopted.

My mommy adopted me
when I was only seven weeks old.

My mommy always gives me good things to eat.

And lots of kisses on the nose!

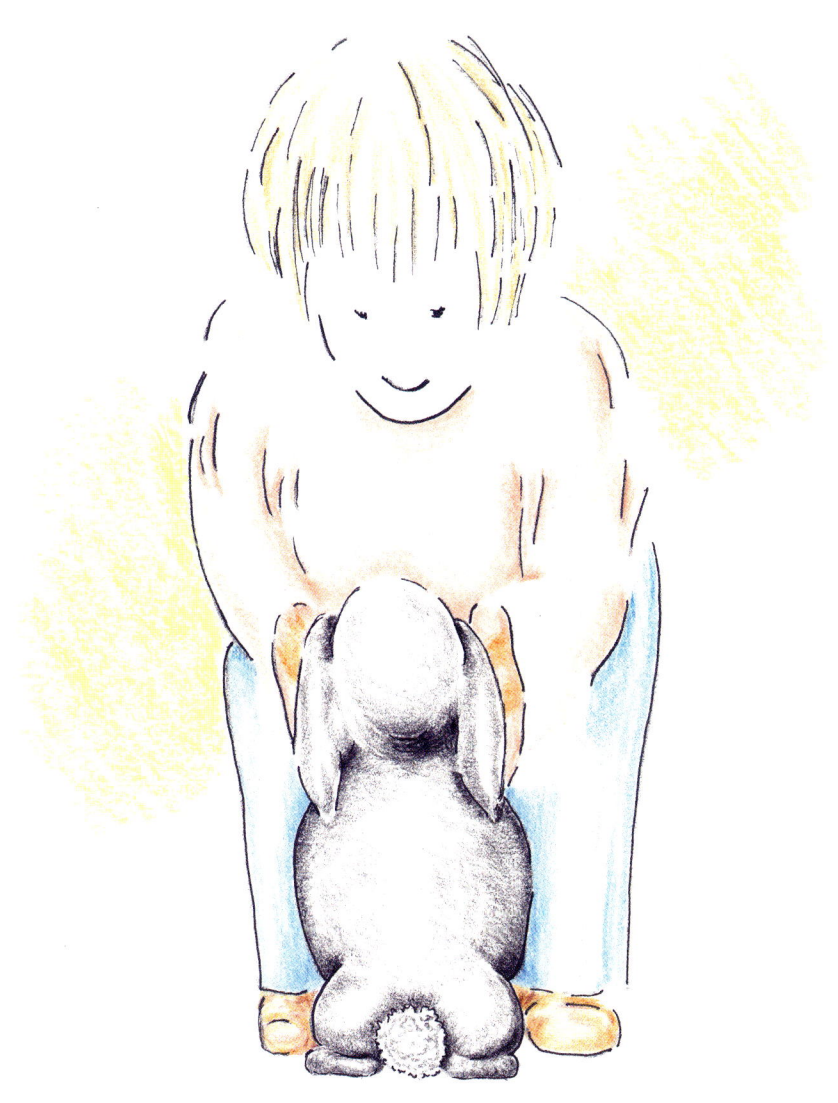

So in return,
I helped Mommy look for God.

Mommy told me that she grew up without any religion and wasn't sure where to look for God.

So we looked for God in books.

We tried to find God by moving around, too, doing yoga exercises.

Then we tried sitting still for hours doing meditation exercises.

Mommy took classes and met some nice people.

But she said that everything just felt the same.
She still couldn't find God and was about to give up.

Then one day I got very sick.

Mommy rushed me to the veterinarian.

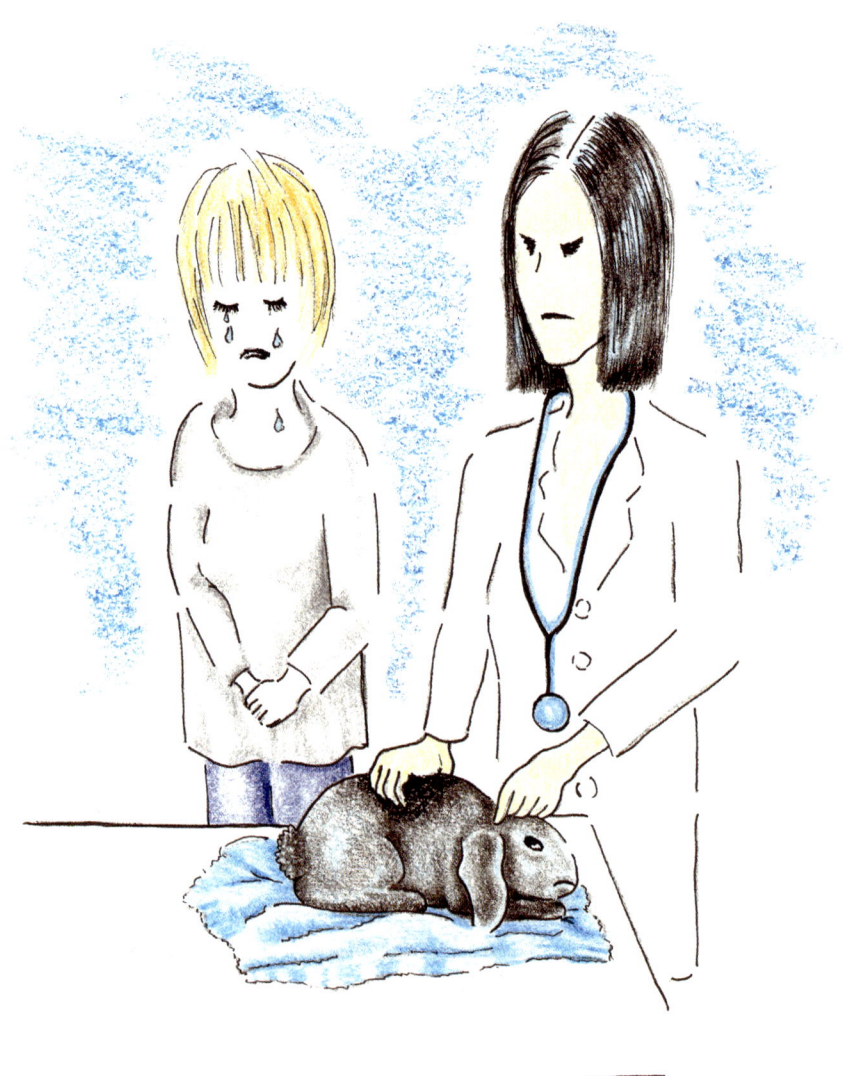

The vet ran some tests
and told Mommy that I might have cancer.

Mommy was so sad.
She held me and cried and cried.

One evening Mommy went walking in a rainstorm.

She heard church bells and followed some people inside.

She lit a candle for me
and started crying and praying . . . and praying . . . and praying.

"Draw near to God and He will draw near to you!" (James 4:8)

And Mommy told me that suddenly the whole church felt warm.

She felt something warm in her heart
and knew that she had found God.

Mommy and I now know that "love is of God; and everyone who loves is born of God and knows God . . . for God is love." (1 John 4:7, 8).

And I got well again!

The vet said she couldn't explain it.

But Mommy and I have learned that
"the prayer of faith will save the sick,
and the Lord will raise him up." (James 5:15)

And . . . after I got well, God adopted Mommy—
just like Mommy adopted me!

"With God all things are possible."
(Matthew 19:26)

About the Author and Illustrator:

Myra T. Johnson ("Mommy") is a social worker with County of Santa Clara Health and Hospital Systems. She resides in San Jose, California, and is a parishioner at Saint Nicholas Antiochian Orthodox Church in San Francisco, California, where she teaches a Sunday School class. A convert to the Orthodox Christian faith in adulthood, she chose the baptismal name "Thecla" in honor of the Protomartyr Thecla, who, when thrown to wild beasts, found that they "snuggled up" against her. This is Myra's first book.

About Snuggles:

Snuggles was a real bunny who shared the author's home and heart for over eleven and a half years. This story is inspired by some actual events which occurred when Snuggles was about six years old. In order to create a story easily understood by young children, some of the time-frames, persons, and places described and depicted in this book have been changed and fictionalized.

About Bunnies:

If you are thinking about adopting a bunny into your family, please contact the House Rabbit Society, a wonderful resource for everything you will need to know about raising a rabbit in a home environment. You can reach the House Rabbit Society online at www.rabbit.org, or by contacting: House Rabbit Society, National Headquarters, 148 Broadway, Richmond, CA 94804; (510) 970-75575.